No Hugs *for* PORCUPiNE

Zoe Waring

RP | KIDS
PHILADELPHIA

Books published by Running Press are available at special discounts for bulk purchases in the United States by corporations, institutions, and other organizations. For more information, please contact the Special Markets Department at Perseus Books, 2300 Chestnut Street, Suite 200, Philadelphia, PA 19103, or call (800) 810-4145, ext. 5000, or e-mail special.markets@perseusbooks.com.

ISBN 978-0-7624-6225-4
Library of Congress Control Number: 2016945292

9 8 7 6 5 4 3 2 1
Digit on the right indicates the number of this printing

Cover and interior design by T.L. Bonaddio
Edited by Julie Matysik
Typography: Bodoni

Published by Running Press Kids,
An Imprint of Perseus Books, LLC.,
A Subsidiary of Hachette Book Group, Inc.

Running Press Book Publishers
2300 Chestnut Street
Philadelphia, PA 19103–4371

Visit us on the web!
www.runningpress.com/rpkids

To all the little Porcupines:
may your day be filled with hugs.

Poor Porcupine couldn't be hugged.

The forest animals, who loved hugging each other, twittered behind Porcupine's back.

"He's too prickly," said Fawn.
"He's so grumpy!" said Rabbit.

Moose, Fox, Beaver, and Owl agreed.
"Who could ever hug Porcupine?" exclaimed Otter.

"I don't need a hug from any of you!"

Porcupine shouted into the echoing forest.

But he *wanted* one.

It was no hugs that made Porcupine grumpy.

He craved a cuddle,

needed a nuzzle,

and searched for
a snuggle.

Dusk crept over the forest. All the animals said their
goodnights, giving each other warm bedtime hugs
before they returned to their burrows, nests, and logs.

All but Porcupine.
He sulked off to his
corner of the forest
and settled on his rock.

Giving his quills a quick shake,
he tried to wrap his little arms around his body.

"Ouch!" he cried.

Even Porcupine couldn't hug Porcupine! He felt extra grumpy.
Porcupine picked up one of his quills from the mossy ground.

Perhaps I can do something about these, he thought.
He tried shaking again,
harder this time.
Only a few quills fell off.

He tried rubbing his back against
a tree to blunt the spikes, but his
quills were sharp as ever.

"Maybe I can cover
myself in moss!"

Porcupine gathered the softest
moss he could find. He lumbered
over to the brook and peered at
his reflection.

"You look silly!" said a voice.
Porcupine turned and spotted Armadillo.
He dropped the moss to the ground.
"That's much better," Armadillo said.

"It's *not* much better,"
said Porcupine, grumpier than before.
"I won't ever get a hug now."

"Cheer up, Porcupine," said Armadillo.
"Would you like a kiss instead?"

"A kiss? What's a kiss?
May I have one, please?" asked Porcupine.

Mwah!
Armadillo pecked a quick kiss on Porcupine's little nose.
"There!" Armadillo said. "That's a kiss."

Porcupine felt happy and warm
and not the least bit grumpy.
He wanted to show all the forest animals
this kiss, but was afraid they
would not give him the chance.

"Don't worry," said Armadillo.
"We can show them together!"

"Okay," mumbled Porcupine, nervously.
And they made their way back through the forest.

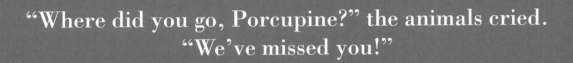

"Where did you go, Porcupine?" the animals cried.
"We've missed you!"

"I was sad," Porcupine muttered,
"because you said I couldn't be hugged."

"It's not that we don't want to
hug you," said Fawn.
"We're just afraid of your
prickly quills."

Armadillo said,
"Well, in that case, Porcupine
could give you a kiss if you
want. Because porcupine kisses
are not prickly!"

"A kiss?" said Rabbit, twitching his nose.
"May I have one, please?" said Otter,
bounding up to Porcupine.

"Sure!" said Porcupine.

Mwah!

"That wasn't prickly at all!" said Otter.
"In fact, it was very nice!"

Porcupine smiled.

"I want a kiss, too,"
whispered Fawn.

"So do I," said Rabbit.

All the forest animals asked
Porcupine if they
could also have a kiss.

So he very carefully planted pecks,

kissed cheeks,

and nudged noses.

Dawn broke over the forest. All the animals said
their good mornings, giving each other quick, sweet kisses
after rising from their burrows, nests, and logs.

All but poor Owl . . .